Dear Mili

Dear Mili

An old tale by Wilhelm Grimm

newly translated by Ralph Manheim

with pictures by Maurice Sendak

Published by Michael di Capua Books

Farrar, Straus and Giroux · New York

For my sister, Natalie
M. S.

Dear Mili,

I'm sure you have gone walking in the woods or in green meadows, and passed a clear, flowing brook. And you've tossed a flower into the brook, a red one, a blue one, or a snow-white one. It drifted away, and you followed it with your eyes as far as you could. And it went quietly away with the little waves, farther and farther, all day long and all night too, by the light of the moon or the stars. It didn't need much light, for it knew the way and it didn't get lost. When it had traveled for three days without stopping to rest, another flower came along on another brook. A child like you, but far far away from here, had tossed it into a brook at the same time. The two flowers kissed, and went their way together and stayed together until they both sank to the bottom. You have also seen a little bird flying away over the mountain in the evening. Perhaps you thought it was going to bed; not at all, another little bird was flying over other mountains, and when all was dark on the earth, the two of them met in the last ray of sunshine. The sun shone bright on their feathers, and as they flew back and forth in the light they told each other many things that we on the earth below could not hear. You see, the brooks and the flowers and the birds come together, but people do not; great mountains and rivers, forests and meadows, cities and villages lie in between, they have their set places and cannot be moved, and humans cannot fly. But one human heart goes out to another, undeterred by what lies between. Thus does my heart go out to you, and though my eyes have not seen you yet, it loves you and thinks it is sitting beside you. And you say: "Tell me a story." And it replies: "Yes, dear Mili, just listen."

There was once a widow who lived at the end of a village; all she had in the world was a little house and the garden that went with it. Her children had died, all but one daughter, whom she loved dearly. She was a dear, good little girl, who was always obedient and said her prayers before going to bed and in the morning when she got up. Everything she did went well. When she planted something in her little garden patch, a clump of violets or a sprig of rosemary, it took root so well that you could see it growing. When danger threatened the little girl, she was always saved, and the mother often thought in her heart: My child must have a guardian angel, who goes everywhere with her, even if the angel cannot be seen.

But it was not God's will that the happy life they led together should continue, for a terrible war overran the whole country. One fine, clear day when mother and child were sitting together outside the house, a great cloud of smoke rose up in the distance and a little while later the heavens resounded with cannon fire. Shouts and tumult rent the air on all sides. "Great God!" cried the mother. "What a fearful storm is coming! Dear child, how shall I save you from the wicked men!"

And, in her great fear, she decided to send the child into the forest, where no enemy could follow. "Come," she said, putting a piece of cake left over from Sunday in the child's pocket. "Come, child. I will take you to the forest. Then go straight ahead until you are quite safe; wait three days and come home; God in His mercy will show you the way."

She took the child to the edge of the forest, kissed her, and let her go.

You can imagine how the child felt at being left all alone. She went deeper and deeper into the forest, the wind blew wildly in the tops of the fir trees, and when thorns took hold of her dress, she was terrified, for she thought that wild beasts had seized her in their jaws and would tear her to pieces. The woodpeckers, crows, and hawks screamed furiously, and at every step sharp stones cut her feet. She trembled with fear, and the farther she went, the heavier grew her heart. The sky clouded over, every trace of blue disappeared, and the storm wind buffeted the branches so hard that they cracked. In the end the dread in her heart grew so great that she could go no further, and she had to sit down. She said to herself: "Oh, dear God, help your child to go on."

Just as she had expected, she felt lighter at heart. Rain began to fall, and she took comfort and said: "God and my heart are weeping together." There she sat until the shower had passed. When she stood up and looked at the sky, she saw little fleecy clouds and the evening sun was shining on them. And she thought: God is feeding His sheep with roses, why would He forget me? So she started off again. Now she was easy in her mind, and I believe it was her guardian angel who, unseen, guided her over cliffs and past deep chasms, for how otherwise could she have come through safely? Most likely the angel had instructed a white dove to fly ahead of the child and show her the way.

At nightfall she came to a plain, where there were no more thorns and no sharp stones, but only soft moss and grass, which soothed her bruised feet. Then one by one the stars came out, and looking up at them the child said: "How bright are the nails on the great door of heaven! What a joy it will be when God opens it!" Then suddenly a star seemed to have fallen to the ground. As the child came nearer, the light grew bigger and bigger until at length she came to a little house and saw that the light was shining from the window.

She knocked at the door and someone cried: "Come in."

When she went in and looked around, she saw an old man sitting there. He said in a friendly voice: "Good evening, dear child, is it you? I've been expecting you a long time." He had a snow-white beard that reached down to the ground, and he looked most venerable and kind. "Sit down, dear child," he said. "You must be tired. Sit in my little chair by the fire and warm yourself." And when she had warmed herself, he said: "You must be hungry and thirsty, I shall give you clear water to drink, but all I have to eat is a few roots that grow in the woods, and you will have to cook them."

The little girl took the roots, scraped them neatly, cooked them over the fire, and added a piece of the Sunday cake, which made them taste good. When the dish was ready, the old man said: "I'm hungry, give me some." The good child gave him more than she kept, but after eating what was left, she felt full.

When they had finished eating, the old man said: "You must be sleepy now. I have only one bed. You sleep in it." "Oh, no," said the child. "A little straw on the floor will be soft enough for me." But the old man picked her up in his arms, put her down on the bed, and covered her. Then she said her prayers and fell asleep.

Early the next morning, when she opened her eyes, the old man was sitting beside the bed and the sun was shining gloriously through the window. "Dear child," he said. "You must get up now and go out to your work; I want you to gather roots for us to eat."

She went happily outside, where she heard more birds singing than she had ever heard before and the flowers round about were so big and beautiful that she had never in all her life seen anything more splendid.

But I suppose you would like to know who the old man with the white beard in the hut was? It was Saint Joseph, who long ago had cared for the Christ Child here on earth; he had known that the good little girl would come to him and had taken her under his protection. It was because he didn't want her to be idle that he had sent her out to work.

All of a sudden, as she was wandering about in the meadows and under the trees, another little girl was standing beside her. The other little girl took her by the hand, showed her where to find the best roots, and helped her dig them up. When they had enough, the other little girl played with her, picked flowers for her, and was very sweet and kind. This little girl had lovely blond hair and a pretty red dress and looked just like the poor little girl, except that her eyes were larger and brighter and she may have been even more beautiful. I'm fairly sure it was her guardian angel, who was allowed, out here in the woods, to let the little girl see her. Again the child cooked the roots and herbs they had gathered, and put in the second piece of her Sunday cake, and again Saint Joseph ate with her.

The third day was no different. As soon as she went outside, the other little girl was there, and they played together in pure joy and glory. Hour after hour went by, and time never hung heavy on their hands. The sky was always bright and there was never a cloud to be seen. And, on the third day, when the child had given up her last piece of cake and the old man had again eaten with her, he said to her: "Dear child, you must go back to your mother now. Your time here is over." "Yes," she said. "I'll be glad to go to my mother, but I'd also like to come back here soon." At that Saint Joseph handed her a rosebud and said: "Never fear. When this rose blooms, you will be with me again."

The other little girl, who was waiting outside the door, took her by the hand and said: "I will lead you by a shorter way. You will be with your mother soon, but you will find the going hard." They started out together and in places where the little girl could not make her way the guardian angel helped her. But in the end she grew so tired that she had to stop. "Oh, if only I had something to refresh me, so I don't faint away before I get to see my mother." At that the guardian angel plucked a white cup-shaped flower that we call bindweed and poured in a few drops of red wine, which revived her and made her strong again. These flowers have had little red stripes ever since.

At the end of the forest the guardian angel pointed to the village and said: "There you will find your mother. She is sitting outside the house, thinking of you. Go now. From here on, you won't be able to see me."

The child went to the village, but it looked strange and unfamiliar to her. In among the houses she knew, there were others she had never seen before; the trees looked different, and there was no trace of the damage the enemy had done. All was peaceful, the grain waved in the breeze, the meadows were green, the trees were laden with fruit. But she had no trouble recognizing her mother's house, and when she came close, she saw an old, old woman with bowed head, sitting on the bench outside the door, enjoying the last rays of the evening sun that hung low over the forest.

The old woman looked up, and when she saw the little girl she cried out in joyful amazement. "Ah, dear child. God has granted my last wish, to see you once again before I die." She kissed her and pressed her to her heart. And then the little girl heard that she had spent thirty years with Saint Joseph in the forest, though to her it had seemed like three days. All the fear and misery her mother had suffered during the great war had passed her by, and her whole life had been just one joyful moment. Her mother had thought wild beasts had torn her to pieces years ago, and yet deep in her heart she had hoped to catch at least a glimpse of her just as she was when she went away. And when she looked up, there stood the dear child, wearing the same little dress.